One Last Wish

A TALE FROM INDIA

Retold by Suzanne I. Barchers
Illustrated by Sue Todd

RED
CHAIR
•PRESS•

Please visit our website at **www.redchairpress.com**.
Find a free catalog of all our high-quality products for young readers.

For a free activity page for this story, go to
www.redchairpress.com and look for Free Activities.

One Last Wish

Publisher's Cataloging-In-Publication Data
(Prepared by The Donohue Group, Inc.)

Barchers, Suzanne I.
One last wish : a tale from India / retold by Suzanne I. Barchers ; illustrated by Sue Todd.
p. : col. ill. ; cm. -- (Tales of honor)
Summary: In this Indian tale, a princess learns a terrible secret about the man she loves,
yet she marries him anyway. Her devotion and persistence pay off when she is granted a
wish, which she uses wisely. Includes special educational sections: Words to know, What
do you think?, and About India.
Interest age level: 006-010.
ISBN: 978-1-937529-76-5 (lib. binding/hardcover)
ISBN: 978-1-937529-60-4 (pbk.)
ISBN: 978-1-936163-92-2 (eBook)
1. Devotion--Juvenile fiction. 2. Princesses--Juvenile fiction. 3. Wishes--Juvenile fiction.
4. Folklore--India. 5. Love--Fiction. 6. Princesses--Fiction. 7. Wishes--Fiction.
8. Folklore--India. I. Todd, Sue. II. Title.

PZ8.1.B37 On 2013

398.2/73/0954   2012951562

This series first published by:
Red Chair Press LLC   PO Box 333   South Egremont, MA 01258-0333

Printed in the United States of America

1 2 3 4 5 18 17 16 15 14

There was once a noble king of a region of India. King Ahapati and his queen were beloved by the people. Their happiness would have been complete if they only had a child. The goddess Lakshmi took pity on them. She told the king in a dream that they would have a child within a year. Sivatra, a beautiful baby girl, was soon born.

Sivatra had a lovely childhood. At age eighteen, she journeyed to the forest to learn from those who lived among nature. After she returned, she spoke to her father.

"My dear father, I met an exiled king named Yumatsena in the forest. An evil king took his throne, leaving him poor and blind. He lives in the forest with his son Sayavan. Father, I have fallen in love with Sayavan."

The king knew that this was an admirable, although unfortunate, family. "Sivatra," he said, "I am delighted that you have chosen such a worthy husband. Before I offer my blessing, however, I want to talk with my counselor."

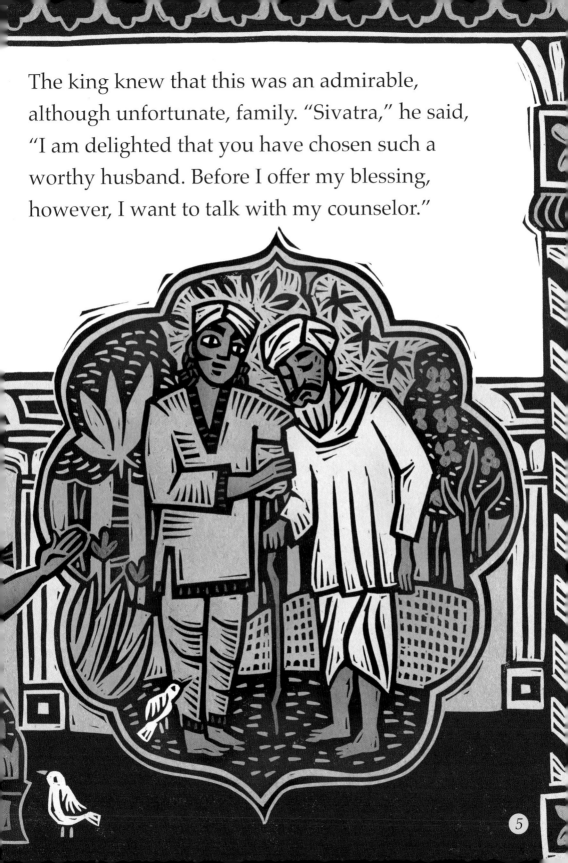

The king called for his counselor, asking if he thought the match was wise.

"My noble king and Sivatra," the counselor replied. "I regret what I must tell you. Last night the goddess Siva spoke to me in a dream. Sayavan has but one year to live. Sivatra, you are doomed to grief if you marry him." The king turned to Sivatra. "Dear daughter, I want your life to be happy. You are too young to be a widow. Find yourself a healthy man."

"Father," Sivatra replied. "It matters not to me how much time we have together. An hour of happiness with my love is worth more to me than a lifetime with another. Just promise that you won't reveal his fate to him."

The king could not deny his daughter her happiness. The wedding was held in the forest where the couple had met. The happy days passed quickly.

Soon there were four days left to the year. Sivatra decided to ask the gods to help. She went to the forest and prayed.

Several hours passed. Sayavan found her and asked why she was standing there.

"My love, I cannot explain," she said. "But I will be here for the next four days and nights."

Sayavan appealed to her, "Sivatra, I don't understand. Please come home."

"No," Sivatra said. "This is something I must do."

Through the long hours, Sivatra prayed, whispering to the gods to grant her a miracle. Soon it was the last sunrise.

Not realizing that this was to be his last day on earth, Sayavan pleaded with her again. "My dear wife, you have not had rest or food for days. Come home and rest while I gather some fruit for you."

Not wanting to miss these last hours together,
Sivatra suggested that they both gather fruit.

After a while, they stopped so that Sayavan could prepare firewood. Sivatra rested and prayed while listening to Sayavan chop wood.

Suddenly he turned to her. "My dear, I can hardly see you. My head hurts dreadfully. I must rest."

He fell into a deep sleep. Sivatra lifted his head into her lap and stroked his forehead. She feared that this was the end.

A moment later, Sivatra looked up to see a frightful figure looming overhead. She eased Sayavan's head onto the ground and stood.

"Who are you? You are not of this world, are you?" she demanded.

"I am Yama, the god of the dead," he said. "I have come for your husband."

Sivatra watched her beloved take his last breath. As Yama turned to leave with Sayavan's soul, she stood in front of him on the path.

"Be gone with you!" he roared. "Go home. His life is over!"

"I will not go home. I will follow him— and you—wherever you go."

Yama had watched her four-day vigil.
He knew she was devoted to Sayavan.

Yama hissed, "I cannot give back his life,
but I can grant one wish. What would it be?"

"Sayavan's father is blind. Can you restore his sight?" Sivatra asked.

"Consider it done. Now, move away," Yama said.

But Sivatra stood on the path, unmoving.

Yama sighed. "Alright. One more wish.
Then you must go."

"Sayavan's father has been exiled for years.
Give him back his empire."

Yama growled, "Done. Now move away."

Sivatra would not leave, though fatigue
pulled at her.

"Make a third wish. Then leave me to my
work," Yama muttered.

"My father has no son. Give him a son,"
Sivatra replied.

Once again he agreed. Once again she would
not move, even though she swayed with
exhaustion.

Yama was annoyed with her persistence.
But he admired her strength.

"Alright, a fourth wish," he said.

"I want a son," Sivatra pleaded.

"So you shall have a son." With that,
he pushed her aside and set off down
the path.

23

Sivatra wept with exhaustion. But she followed him down the path.

"Please," she begged. "Just one more wish. One more. Please..."

Yama stopped and faced her. "Your devotion baffles me. I'll give you one last wish, whatever you desire."

"Give my husband back to me!" she cried.

"You will never give up, will you? Enough!
It is done." And with that he disappeared.

Sivatra ran back to her husband. His color returned and his eyes fluttered open.

"What has happened? Was I asleep?" he asked.

"You were just resting. Let's go home, my dear."

The young couple returned to their home, only to find Yumatsena there with the news that he could see once again. A short time later a messenger arrived, announcing that the evil king had been overthrown. Yumatsena was king once again. And Sivatra shared the news that she was expecting a child.

"This is truly a day of miracles," Yumatsena declared.

Sivatra looked at her husband and whispered, "Yes, it is. One only has to believe."

exiled: kept away from one's home country or lands

fatigue: extreme tiredness

noble: having fine personal and moral qualities

persistence: firm in action in spite of difficulty or opposition

vigil: a period of staying awake when normally asleep

WHAT DO YOU THINK?

Question 1:   How did Sivatra feel when she learned the man she loved had one year to live? Describe what she did or said then.

Question 2:   Do you think Sayavan knew he had only a year to live? Why or why not?

Question 3:   Yama said he would grant Sivatra one wish. Why do you think she was granted more wishes?

Question 4:   This is a story about devotion. What are other words that can be used to describe the theme of this story?

About India

The long and colorful history of India is one of dynasties and mysteries. *One Last Wish* is a tale most likely from the Classical Age of India between the 7th and 13th Centuries. This period produced some of India's finest art and was important in the spiritual development of Buddhism and Hinduism. The goddess Lakshmi is a Hindu deity celebrated during the Diwali festival of lights.

About the Author

After fifteen years as a teacher, Suzanne Barchers began a career in writing and publishing. She has written over 100 children's books, two college textbooks, and more than 20 reader's theater and teacher resource books. She previously held editorial roles at Weekly Reader and LeapFrog and is on the PBS Kids Media Advisory Board. Suzanne also plays the flute professionally – and for fun – from her home in Stanford, CA.

About the Illustrator

Sue Todd is an award-winning illustrator living in Toronto, Canada. She creates linocut prints in her yellow studio, and gets her best ideas while riding around the city on her bicycle.